Justus Henry Christian Helmuth, Adam Seybert

An Inaugural Dissertation

being an attempt to disprove the doctrine of the putrefaction of the blood

of living animals - submitted to the examination of the Rev. John Ewing,

S.T.P. provost

Justus Henry Christian Helmuth, Adam Seybert

An Inaugural Dissertation
being an attempt to disprove the doctrine of the putrefaction of the blood of living animals - submitted to the examination of the Rev. John Ewing, S.T.P. provost

ISBN/EAN: 9783337394851

Printed in Europe, USA, Canada, Australia, Japan

Cover: Foto ©Andreas Hilbeck / pixelio.de

More available books at **www.hansebooks.com**

AN
INAUGURAL DISSERTATION:
BEING AN

ATTEMPT

TO DISPROVE THE DOCTRINE OF THE

PUTREFACTION OF THE BLOOD

O F

LIVING ANIMALS.

SUBMITTED TO THE EXAMINATION OF THE

REV. JOHN EWING, S. T. P. PROVOST;

THE TRUSTEES, AND MEDICAL PROFESSORS OF THE
UNIVERSITY OF PENNSYLVANIA,

FOR THE DEGREE OF DOCTOR OF MEDICINE;

On the 8th. day of May, A. D. 1793.

BY ADAM SEYBERT, OF PHILADELPHIA;

*Honorary Member of the Philadelphia, and Member of the
American, Medical Societies.*

"FOR THE LIFE OF THE FLESH IS IN THE BLOOD."
Leviticus.

PHILADELPHIA:
PRINTED BY T. DOBSON, AT THE STONE-HOUSE,
NO. 41, SOUTH SECOND-STREET.

M,DCC,XCIII.

To CASPAR WISTAR, M. D.

ADJUNCT PROFESSOR OF ANATOMY, SURGERY, AND MID-
WIFERY IN THE *UNIVERSITY* OF *PENNSYLVANIA.*

SIR,

IN addreffing this Inaugural Differtation to you, every
body that knows you will readily admit the peculiar propriety of the tribute. Your juftly acknowledged abilities
leave no room to doubt that I have an intereft in making
this offering. But, whilft I candidly admit this, I feel
and confefs profound obligations of gratitude to a belov-
ed mafter, for his very beneficial inftructions, and his many
courtefies and attentions. To whom can the following
production, with more evident propriety, be infcribed,
than to him who planted the Seed of Knowledge, and,
with anxious folicitude, fuperintended the growth ?—To
you, Sir, I am indebted for whatever progrefs I may
have made in Medical Science; and I am ambitious, that
the firft fruits of my labors fhould be prefented to the
world under the adorning fanction of your patronage.

The cordiality of your friendfhip has naturally infpired
me with fentiments of efteem and attachment, which it
will ever be my pride, as it is my duty and intereft, to
cherifh.

Believe me, Sir, nothing can ever obliterate from my
mind the mingled fentiments of gratitude and efteem with
which I remain

Your obliged friend and Pupil,

A. SEYBERT.

INTRODUCTION.

THE Opinion, that the blood became putrid in many Difeafes, is of ancient date. It has been embraced, with various modifications by moſt of the fcƐts in Medicine. It particularly engaged the attention and belief of the learned Boerhaave, who publicly taught it in the celebrated fchool of Leyden. Under the impofing authority of his name, and by means of his induſtry, it was diffuſed throughout almoſt the whole globe. It became the theme of the vulgar ; and at this day has many great and illuſtrious names to fupport it.

There have been, however, at different times, a few Medical Philofophers, who, although they adopted it in fome inſtances, feem to have had doubts refpecting the truth of the doctrine, and to have rejected it in their explanations of many difeafes. In this clafs may be reckoned the celebrated Hoffmann, who explained the phænomena of many diſorders without any regard to the ſtate of the blood : He was followed in this by the great Cullen, who, in his fyſtem, attends lefs to the ſtate of the fluids in difeafes than any of his predeceffors. The doctrine has of late been wholly denied by the very ingenious Dr. Milman in his treatife on the Scurvy ; and entirely rejected by the late fagacious Dr. Brown of Edinburgh, from his Syſtem of Medicine. Many phyficians appear to have adopted the fentiments of thefe gentlemen ; fo that at prefent there

2

is

is a diverſity of opinion among medical philoſophers reſpecting the Putrefaction of the Blood of *Living Animals*.

On examining the ſubject, I found that it had never been put to the teſt of fair experiment ; but, that ſpeculative reaſoning (too often deluſive at beſt) and a few indeciſive facts, were the chief ſupports of the argument on both ſides. With theſe data, the reſult was neither ſatisfactory nor convincing. I then determined to contribute my mite towards inveſtigating the matter by experiment. In the proſecution of this attempt, my attention has been directed to the advancement of Science ; and, in the detailing of the Experiments which I have made with this view, truth ſhall be my polar ſtar.

I have been induced from reflection and experiment to adopt a poſitive belief on this ſubject, and to deny the truth of the doctrine which I have juſt noticed. I am, therefore, neceſſarily led into an oppoſition to the opinions of many celebrated men. But, I truſt, I have obſerved a decent regard and veneration for thoſe from whom I differ, without being at all depreſſed by the weight of their authority. Having viewed nature *attentively*, I ſhall endeavour to communicate *accurately* what I have obſerved. I will not ſacrifice truth to the luſtre of great names, but, with confidence adopt the ſentiment of Cicero—" Mea fuit ſemper hæc in hac re voluntas et ſententia, quemvis ut hoc mallem de iis, qui eſſent idonei, ſuſcipere quam me : me, ut mallem quam neminem."

INAUGURAL DISSERTATION.

IT will be proper, before I enter upon the confideration of the Putrefaction of the Blood of living Animals, to take a brief view of *Putrefaction in general*; for, this is, indeed, the only method by which we can be prepared for an examination of the circumftances neceffary to induce that ftate of the blood in living animals.

Though Chemiftry is much improved, and numerous difcoveries are made almoft every day, by different philofophers, *Putrefaction* is, at this moment confidered as the fame difficult fubject, that it was in the days of the celebrated *Lord Bacon*.

This laft ftage of Fermentation, in the days of Stahl, was fuppofed to be a mere confequence of the *vinous* and *acetous* ftages; but, modern difcoveries teach us the contrary; for we find, that while fome fubftances undergo only the laft ftage, others fuffer the three fucceffive changes in a regular manner: thus mucilages, &c. become acid without undergoing the vinous fermentation, and the glutinous matter of vegetables will putrefy before it undergoes either of the other changes.

Obfervation,

Obfervation, the grand parent of difcovery, has taught us, that no fubftance is capable of undergoing a change by the putrefactive fermentation, except it be *animal* or *vegetable* ; and that the numerous claffes of the productions of nature, comprehended under the title of the Mineral Kingdom, are excluded. It is alfo an opinion, generally eftablifhed, and proved by experiment, that the fluid and fofter parts of thofe bodies, putrefy much fooner than the harder and more folid parts. It has likewife been obferved, " That the flefh of younger animals is fomewhat more prone to putridity, than that of older animals."*

Animal and vegetable matters cannot putrefy in every fituation or condition in which they may exift ; for it is neceffary that a living animal or vegetable fhould undergo a confiderable change, before it can be rendered capable thereof : It muft even be deprived of life, or the vital principle. No one has ever feen an entire animal or vegetable putrefy whilft alive ; and Beccher, on this fubject, beautifully obferves : " Caufa putrefactionis primaria defectus fpiritus vitalis balfamini eft." And, indeed, in all refearches into thofe kingdoms which are the fubjects of *fermentation*, it is of fo great confequence to keep this univerfal actuating principle in view, that by neglecting it, we may commit great miftakes, and look to other caufes than the true ones for its palpable effects ; infomuch that the learned Chaptal, when regretting the imperfect fuccefs which Chemiftry has met with, in the analyfis of animal matters, cannot help obferving it. " All (fays he) have miftaken or overlooked that principle of life which inceffantly acts upon the folids and fluids, modifies, without ceafing, the impreffion of external objects ; impedes the

* Medical Commentaries, Vol. II. p. 142.

the degenerations which depend on the conftitution itfelf;
and prefents to us. phænomena which chemiftry never
could have known or predicted by attending to the invari-
able laws obferved in inanimate bodies."*

The prefence of that invifible elaftic fluid, which we
term *vital air*, is fo neceffary to putrefaction, that a body
cannot putrefy without being in contact with it; and
may be preferved found and pure for years if the commu-
nication between them be deftroyed. It is a well known
fact that a body will not putrefy *in vacuo*: This has been
noticed by an ingenious author in the following words:
" How much the air contributes to putrefaction, is evident hence, that bodies buried deep under the earth, or
in water, out of the reach of air, fhall remain for ages
entire; which yet, being expofed to the open air, fhall
foon rot and moulder away."†

It appears that too great a degree of moifture, or a to-
tal want of it, retards the procefs of putrefaction. In order, therefore, that a body may putrefy, it is neceffary
that it be only duly moiftened. Thus it happens, that
after an animal or vegetable fubftance has been made perfectly dry, it may be preferved, in that ftate, for many
years after. It has been obferved by the immortal Beccher, that too great a degree of moifture prevents putrefaction: Thefe are his words: " Nimia quoque humiditas
a putrefactione impedit, prout nimius calor; nam corpora
in aqua potius gradatim confumi quam putrefcere, fi nova
femper affluens fit, experientia docet: unde longo tempore
integra

* Chaptal's Chemiftry, Vol. III. p. 280,
† Frewen's Phyfiologia, p. 128.

integra interdum fubmerfa prorfus a putrefactione immunia
vidimus; adeo ut nobis aliquando fpeculatio occurreret,
tractando tali modo cadavera anatomiæ fubjicienda, quo
diutius a fœtore et putrefactione immunia forent."*

That *all* enlivening principle, *heat*, which, in a certain
degree, is neceffary to life, is no lefs neceffary to the
bringing on of the diffolution of a body. Temperature
has been found to have great influence in promoting and
retarding putrefaction.

I have now mentioned the moft effential circumftances
neceffary to promote the inception of putrefaction; to
which we may fubjoin *Reft*; for bodies do not putrefy
while in continual motion. In proportion as thefe circumftances take place the procefs will advance with
greater or leffer rapidity.

Certain fubftances, as well known to the vulgar as to
the philofopher, by the name of Ferments, when added
to a fermentable mafs, are found to haften the procefs in
a manner truly aftonifhing; though both the peafant and
the philofopher ftand on an equal footing with regard to
a knowledge of the principle by which their application
produces a fpecific operation. "We are told indeed (fays
the ingenious Mr. Henry) that a vinous ferment induces
the vinous, that a ferment of an acetous kind brings on
the acetous fermentation, and a putrid one, that fermentation which ends in putrefaction. But we receive no
more information, relative to the manner in which they
produce thofe effects, than we do with regard to fermentation itfelf."†

I will

* Phyf. Sub. lib. 1. f. 5. cap. 1. p. 277.
† Manchefter Memoirs, Vol. II. p. 259.

I will now proceed to examine, whether, in becoming putrid, a body undergoes any confiderable change; and, whether it be poffible to remove putrefcency after it has taken place.

The very meaning of the word *putrefaction* conveys the idea that an effential change muft have taken place in any fubftance which has acquired a putrid ftate.

Putrefaction reduces both animals and vegetables to the fame principles, for, it caufes an entire and complete decompofition of them, infomuch that it is difficult, and indeed impoffible, to diftinguifh between a putrefied mafs of animal and one of vegetable matter. The former characteriftics of each are at an end. Colour, texture, and every fenfible quality of the body, are thereby deftroyed. It reduces the animate part of the Creation to an indifcriminate level with inanimate matter. There is abundance of truth in the obfervation, that bodies, in this procefs, undergo a new combination, as well as feparation of their conftituent parts. Putrefaction caufes the fweeteft fubftances to become the moft offenfive and difagreeable to the fmell; and, inftead of a vegetable acid, at length produces a volatile alkali—bodies poffeffing very oppofite principles.

Many philofophers have gone fo far as to fay, that, by certain chemical proceffes, they were able not only to render putrid fubftances fweet again, but reftore them to the condition they were in, previoufly to their undergoing this peculiar change. This, according to them, is to to be effected by furrounding the putrefied body with an atmofphere of fixed air; to the lofs of which principle, an
enlightened

enlightened philofopher wholly attributed the changes produced in a body by putrefaction ; though the opinion has been ingenioufly refuted, and therefore needs not much confideration in this place *.

It is true, that by furrounding a putrefied body with fixed air, we fhall prevent the advancement of the procefs ; yet the fixed air has no fpecific operation in this refpect, for other fubftances poffefs a fimilar property. After I had fuffered feveral pieces of highly putrid beef to remain completely covered with frefh pump water for feveral hours, and then wafhed them frequently in water feveral times renewed, I found, that by this operation the water gained a highly offenfive and putrid fmell, and that the meat had loft a great degree of its own ; but its folidity was not in the leaft reftored. It is a common and well-known fact in domeftic œconomy, that meat, which has become tainted, is very frequently wafhed in frefh water before it is cooked ; and the reafon affigned for this procefs is, that the meat is thereby rendered fweeter, Thus do houfe-keepers reafon from a knowledge of the fact without any theory to bias them.

Hence it appears very clear, that to explain this fact no fpecific operation is neceffary to be recurred to, fince water, free from the combination of fixed air, had effects fimilar to thofe produced by fixed air itfelf. Mr. Chaptal, in my opinion, explains the operation of this, and of the other fubftances which are faid to have the like effect, upon very fimple and philofophical principles. When fpeaking of the neceffity of the prefence of vital air to putrefaction,

* Medical Commentaries, Vol. II. p. 150.

putrefaction, he fays, " We fhall obferve, on this fubject, that the effects obferved in flefh expofed to the Carbonic acid, Nitrogene gas, &c. are referable to a fimilar caufe; and it appears to me that it is without fufficient proof that a conclufion has been drawn, that thefe fame gafes, internally taken, ought to be confidered as antifeptic; becaufe, in the cafes we have mentioned, they act only by defending the bodies they furround from the contact of vital air, which is the principle of putrefaction *."

To me it appears plain, that, fo great is the chemical change and decompofition which a putrid body has un-dergone, that no means can remedy it. On this point Fontana truly obferves, " We do not know any power, nature herfelf does not difclofe any, that can recompofe an organ that is deftroyed, and entirely decompofed by putrefaction, or by the concuffions of external bodies. This is what has never yet either been accomplifhed or feen. We have, therefore, every poffible reafon not only to believe an animal that is reduced to this ftate dead, but likewife to believe it dead for ever †."

From the above confideration of putrefaction, as going on out of the body, it appears, that a certain degree of heat, the prefence of vital air, a certain degree of moif-ture, together with reft, are indifpenfably neceffary to putrefaction; and that without their prefence no body can putrefy. We alfo know, that by adding certain fub-ftances to bodies which are to undergo the change, the procefs is haftened in a manner furprifing to every one who has ever had occafion to notice it.

Having

---

* Chaptal's Chemiftry, Vol. III. p. 398.
† Fontana on Poifons, Vol. I. p. 406.

Having confidered the circumftances in which fermentation, in general, takes place, as it is conceivable that if the above circumftances be prefent in the living animal, the procefs might readily go on in it—let us examine if thefe neceffary requifites be prefent, fo as to act in a due and proper manner upon that vital fluid, *the blood*.

Several queftions occur here.—Is there any difference between dead and living matter?—Is there not in living animals a pofitive power of refifting putrefaction?—Whether the nice and inexplicable operation which is employed in converting the dull mafs of the motionlefs creation into the peculiar condition of organic fenfibility, acts to no purpofe?—In fact, whether the principal characteriftic of death, has not been determined by phyfiologifts to be the beginning of putrefaction in the body?

The principle we denominate *vital*, with whofe effects we begin to be acquainted, though its nature and origin will perhaps ever be hidden from us, is found to be the chief impediment to the putrefaction of a living animal. As foon as the animal is deprived of it, putrefaction is the inevitable confequence, except the above precautions be well obferved. This may be fairly demonftrated. All the circumftances neceffary to putrefaction take place with refpect to the external furface of our bodies, yet they do not putrefy while alive; but if life be by any means deftroyed, they will as readily undergo the procefs as other inanimate matter.

It is to be obferved, that by the living principle is underftood that power which in an animal actuates its whole fyftem, or from which is derived fenfation, moti-

3   on,

on, and the other qualities of life. It is the caufe of the prefervation of the body from diffolution, and is capable of exifting, for fometime, under a fufpenfion of all its actions *.

We will now proceed to confider the prefence of *heat*, pure *air*, *moifture*, and *reft*, with regard to the blood; in order to determine whether we might expect a putrefaction of that fluid if the principle of life, were not alone fufficient to obviate it.

1ft. Of Heat. Though different degrees of heat are found fufficient to maintain life, in different animals, yet no animal while alive has ever been found devoid of a confiderable quantity of it; indeed, fo careful was nature in this refpect, that fhe has endowed man, and the inferior animals, with a power, whereby they are capable of generating heat ;—a procefs the inveftigation of which has of late much engaged the attention of philofophers, and upon which confiderable light has been thrown. It is probable that the blood of every living animal contains a degree of heat fufficient to fupport the procefs of putrefaction.

2dly. Pure Air. That element fo neceffary to our exiftence, and which we receive into our bodies, by means of thofe vital vifcera, the lungs, is no lefs neceffary to the maintaining of animal life, than to the procefs of putrefaction. A man will no more live, than a dead body will purefy, in vacuo †.

C

It

---

* Gardiner's Animal Economy, p. 3.

† That air is a very active and powerful agent in putrefaction, is evident from the following fact, viz. Whilft pus remains fhut up

in

It was for a long time fuppofed that elaftic air exifted
in the blood-veffels of living animals ; but, the experiments of the ingenious Darwin clearly prove the contrary ; the following is one of them. " Part of the jugular vein of a fheep, full of blood, was included between
two tight ligatures, and cut out while the animal was yet
alive. It was immediately put into a glafs of warm water,
and placed in the receiver of an air pump. It funk at firft
to the bottom of the water, and did not rife again, although
the air was carefully exhaufted. After this, it was wiped
dry, and laid on the brafs floor of the receiver. The air
was again exhaufted, but there was not the leaft vifible
expanfion of the vein or its contents *."

By the experiments above referred to it is reduced to a
certainty, that no air exifts, formally in the blood, while
enclofed in the blood-veffels. And it is evident, that it
was without fufficient grounds, that philofophers infer-
red, that air exifted in the blood, while enclofed in the
blood-veffels ; becaufe they perceived it in blood drawn
from a vein, and placed in the receiver of an air pump ;
for during its expofure it muft have had time to abforb
air from the atmofphere.

The celebrated Huxham was of opinion, that, " elaftic
air is probably generated in the arterial and venous fyf-
tems,

in a perfectly clofe cavity it will keep fweet and inodorous, but on
expofure to the atmofphere, it contracts in a very fhort time a putrid fmell ; the fame circumftance takes place with regard to extravafated blood.

* Medical Commentaries, Vol. VI. p. 35.

tems, in putrid fevers *," though he has no experiments to prove it. Let us then examine, whether air can exift in the blood-veffels of living animals.

With this view the ingenious Luzuriaga tried many experiments on living dogs. He injected feveral different kinds of air into the blood-veffels, and in every inftance the animals were killed, in a very fhort time. I will only mention that he twice injected inflammable air ; once phlogifticated air ; once fixed air ; once nitrous air. I will ftate the particular circumftances that happened in the inftance, when dephlogifticated or pure air, which is the chief agent of putrefaction, was injected.—It was forced into the jugular vein of a dog, and in three minutes he died. On diffection, the blood appeared of a lively red colour, and frothy, but not grumous nor coagulated †.

Thus it appears, that air does not, and cannot exift, formally, in the blood-veffels of a living animal ; a circumftance which refutes the opinion, that the blood is capable of undergoing the procefs of of putrefaction, during the life of the animal.

3dly. Moifture. No perfon in his fenfes dares to deny the prefence of this third circumftance, as effential to putrefaction, and therefore it needs no further confideration.

4thly. We have mentioned that it was neceffary for a body, which is to undergo the putrefactive procefs, to be at reft. The continual motion of the blood of living
animals,

---

* Medical Qbfervations, Vol. III. p. 36.
† Luzuriaga's Inaug. Differtat. Eden. 1786, p. 26.

animals, muſt certainly be a great impediment to the pro-
ceſs ; and indeed motion has been found to be a very effectual means of preventing it ; even a briſk wind has been
known to retard it *.

We have found that the life of the animal, the want of
air in the blood-veſſels, and its circulatory motion, were
great impediments to the putrefaaction of the blood ; we
ſhall now proceed to conſider, whether the principle of
animal life is contained in the blood.

The ſituation of that principle, to which we owe our
exiſtence as living beings, is at preſent much diſputed.
While ſome Phyſiologiſts will have it to exiſt wholly in
the nervous ſyſtem, in the form of a ſubtle fluid, whoſe
preſence the beſt microſcopes have not been able to diſco-
ver ; there are others, whoſe authority is by no means inferior, who ſtrenuouſly oppoſe the doctrine, and perſiſt that
blood partakes of it alſo. In this latter claſs we may rank
the celebrated Hunter and Fontana.

That the life of the animal exiſts in the blood, is an
opinion of as ancient a date as Holy Writ itſelf : It was the
favourite ſentiment of many ancient philoſophers ; and the
great Harvey, to whom we are ſo much indebted, ſays,
" the blood is the primum vivens, and the ultimum mori-
ens, of the animal."

This hypotheſis was for ſometime ſunk into oblivion, but
was again revived and placed on a firm baſis by the able
Mr. John Hunter of London ; who ſupports the doctrine
by

* Medical Commentaries, Vol. II. p. 146.

by reafoning truly philofophical, and by experiments, in my opinion, incontrovertibly convincing. It would be needlefs for me to repeat all the ingenious arguments which are made ufe of by him on this occafion, as they may be eafily feen, by referring to the Encyclopædia, Vol. III. p. 313.

His 5th argument alone would almoft fuffice to convince me of the truth of his opinion. " The blood (fays he) preferves life in the different parts of the body. When the nerves going to a part are tied or cut, the part becomes paralytic, and loofes all power of motion ; but it does not mortify ; if the artery be cut, the part dies, and mortification enfues. What keeps it alive in the firft place ? Mr. Hunter believes it is the living principle which alone can keep it alive ; and he thinks that this phenomenon is inexplicable on any other fuppofition, than that life is fupported by the blood"*.

This doctrine is every day gaining ground ; and appears to be further fupported by the opinions and experiments, of the celebrated Fontana ; who obferves, " What may lead one to fufpect, that a very active and volatile principle does really exift in the blood, is, that the vipers venom prevents its coagulation when it is drawn from the veffels, and on the contrary, produces it in the veffels themfelves. One would fuppofe (fays he) in the firft cafe, that fomething had flown off from the blood, which exifts in it when it is enclofed by the veffels" †.

" My experiments on animals (continues this laft mentioned enlighted philofopher) in which the nerves were bit
by

* Encyclopædia Loc. citat.
† Fontana on Poifons, Vol. II. p. 135.

by vipers, shew that the venom is a substance perfectly inno-
cent to these organs, that it does not occasion in them any
sensible change, and that they are not even a means or vehi-
cle of conveying it to the animal. In a word, it appears
that the nervous system does not concur more to the production of the diseases of the venom, than does the ten-
don, or any other insensible part of the animal : on the
other hand, all the experiments on the blood, the injection of venom into the vessels, and so soon constantly
evince that the action of the venom of the viper is on the
blood itself. This fluid is alone changed by the venom,
and this fluid conveys the venom to the animal, and distri-
butes it to its whole body. The action of the venom, and
its effects on the blood, are almost instantaneous."*

His experiments, in my opinion, allow this inference,
that since life was not destroyed by the immediate application of the poison to the bare nerves, and that the loss of
it was almost instantaneous when the poison was applied
to the blood ; there exists some quality in the blood, that
does not exist in the nerves ; and as death can only be produced by destroying the vital principle, this principle must
consequently exist in the blood, and in a state different
from that in which it exists in the nervous system.

. I will now proceed to give a connected view of the rea-
sons, which together with the experiments hereafter to be
mentioned, induce me to deny the putrefaction of the blood
to have ever taken place, and which confirm me in believing, that no such change can happen in the blood of living animals.

1st. We

* Fontana on Poisons, Vol. I, p. 396.

1ft. We have feen that the procefs of putrefaction cannot take place in the animal or vegetable kingdoms, until
after the animal or plant be deprived of life. I think we
have given fome proof of the blood's containing the principle of Animal Life, of which (whether it be convincing
or not) the candid will judge.   When life is once perfectly
deftroyed, there are no means, at our command, by which
it can be again reftored: therefore, we muft infer, that
all putrid cafes are neceffarily mortal, or a putrefaction of
the blood cannot take place.

2dly. From viewing the procefs of mortification, as going on in the folid parts of animals—for the death of the
part *invariably* precedes the fymptoms of putrefcency, as
is evidenced by the want of fenfibility in the part.

3dly. There is no vital air in the blood-veffels, and we
know putrefaction cannot go on without it.

4thly. The blood in the living animal is in continual
motion—a fmall degree of motion has been known to im-
pede the procefs.

5thly. The doctrine of ferments. For as long as a
drop of this putrid blood remained in the veffels, no particle could exift in them, without being changed by it ;
therefore it is a neceffary confequence, that in every cafe,
where putrefaction is fuppofed to have taken place in the
blood, every drop of that fluid fhould be drawn from the
veffels, and the veffels fhould undergo a perfect cleanfing
before healthy blood could exift in them ; confequently,
if the veffels are not cleanfed, the procefs muft neceffarily

continue

continue for ever, and in attempting to cleanfe them; would not death be the inevitable confequence ? *

6thly. We are as yet unacquainted with any means by which we are able to recover a body, when once putrid; for, according to a chemical axiom, it has undergone a perfect decompofition in the procefs ; and, certainly, without obviating the effects of putrefaction on the blood, and reducing it to its former ftate, the animal cannot exift for any length of time.

7thly. In every cafe of putrefaction a great quantity of elaftic air is evolved, and no author (as far as I know) has made mention of the prefence of air in the blood-veffels of thofe who have died of difeafes, which were fuppofed to belong to the putrid clafs, and whofe bodies were diffected immediately after death. It has been fairly proved that air, on being injected into the veffels, kills in a very fhort time †.

8thly. According to the ideas of the fupporters of the putrefaction of the blood in difeafes, the procefs muft be

4   different

---

* The difficulty of reftraining putrefaction after it has taken place, and of deftroying the putrid ferment in veffels that have contained putrid fubftances, is well known to the brewers. When their liquor becomes putrid, or as they term it, " foxed," the veffels which contained it become fo contaminated, that they will excite the fame fermentation in any frefh liquor that may be put into them, even after they are wafhed. It is only by whitewafhing or fcouring them with lime that they can be thoroughly cleanfed. I have heard of a brewer, who was fo much embarraffed by a putrid ferment in his veffels, that he was about giving up his bufinefs, when he fortunately learned the ufe of lime.

† Vide ante Page 19.

different in Typhus, &c. from what it is in fcurvy; fince, in the former cafe, bark and wine, together with other ftimuli, are the only true remedies; whereas, according to them, thefe remedies are found to be of little or no fervice in the latter, and frefh vegetables are its only remedies. For the blood, they fay, is putrid in both inftances; and fince putrefaction going on in the fame fubftance would appear to be always the fame, we might, with propriety fuppofe, that, what retards and corrects it in the one inftance, would do it in the other. Who has thought of exhibiting ~~fuch~~ *fresh* vegetables, in typhus, yellow fever, &c. and neglecting thofe powerful remedies, bark and wine?

9thly. It is incompatible with found reafoning to fuppofe that putrefaction of the blood takes place in the plague, &c. fince we find that perfons fometimes fall down dead, immediately on being expofed to the effluvia, that have been faid to give origin to this and other difeafes of the fame clafs, as the porters, who opened bales of goods in the lazarettos of Marfeilles. Mead relates, that, "Upon opening one of the bales of wool in a field, two Turks employed in the work were immediately killed, and fome birds which happened to fly over the place, dropped down dead *." How is it poffible that the mafs of blood, or any part of it, could become in the leaft degree putrid in thofe inftances? For the fpace of time, before death was produced, was too fhort to allow of it. Since the poifon kills fo quickly, can we with reafon fuppofe that an animal can live while the fountain of life is impregnated with it? If a fmall portion of fuch effluvia produces difeafe, when its action

D   may,

* Mead's Works, p. 198.

may, exclufively, be fuppofed to be merely on the external furface of the body, Is there not ftrong ground for believing that inftant death would follow if the blood were
in the leaft tainted by it ?

10thly. Experiments feem to prove, that the blood is
peculiarly qualified to excite motion in the heart and ar-
teries, and that no other fluid will anfwer the fame purpofe.—That even milk, and other bland liquors, when injected into the veffels of living animals, kill. We know
it is an eftablifhed truth, that by putrefaction bodies undergo a complete decompofition and diffolution of their
of their conftituent parts, and are rendered totally different from what they were before—How then can we ima-
gine that life can be kept up whilft the blood is in a putrid ftate in the veffels ?

For thefe reafons I concluded that a putrefaction of the
blood could not take place in the living body : but the
importance of the fubject induced me to engage in a fe-
ries of Experiments which might enable me, with more
indifputable certainty, to decide the queftion, Whether
the blood of living animals can be rendered putrid ?

And this I fuppofe, if poffible, would be afcertained
by the following circumftances, viz.

I. By Starvation.

II. By a putrid Diet.

And, III. by injecting putrid and other fubftances into
blood-veffels.

1ft. Of

1ft. Of Starvation. When we confider the many and various actions performed by man and other animals, we plainly fee why a certain quuntity of aliment is neceffary to be taken by them. Phyfiology teaches, that by every action man fuffers a lofs of the folids, and that by every fecretion the blood becomes lefs in quantity.

The blood being the fountain from whence all the fo-lid parts derive their fupport, and the fluids their origin, it muft naturally have been fuppofed to be affected by ftarvation, as it is immediately prepared from the aliment we take in.

If the cafe be as above ftated, is it not furprifing that man can live for a length of time without taking any nou-rifhment at all? There are inftances related where men have lived for fix, twelve, and even fourteen days, or longer, without receiving any aliment *.

Drink is found to be no lefs neceffary to the maintain-ing of animal life than the folid matters of our food. The neceffity of this article was fuppofed to be merely in recruiting, blunting, and correcting the acrimony of the blood which would take place if we did not ufe them. And it has been found by experiment, that life may be fupported a much longer time by water than it could with-out it. Rhedi, who made experiments to afcertain how much longer life might be fupported by the ufe of drink, without the ufe of any other article of diet, than when the animal was totally deprived of all food, found, that fowls to whom he gave no drink lived until the ninth day ; whereas

* Manchefter Memoirs, Vol. II. p. 467. and feq.

whereas one who was allowed water, lived more than twenty days *.

Though man may live for a confiderable length of time, without taking in any nourifhment, yet his fituation is not agreeable ; for, he not only fuffers pain, but all the functions, as well bodily as mental, are in confequence affected ; his fenfations are ftrange, his ideas confufed, his fight deceptive and deranged, his countenance becomes pale and fallow, his weight decreafes confiderably, though the excretions are fparing or none at all, the refpiration fuffers, the action of the heart decreafes in proportion, till at laft no pulfation can be felt, debility by degrees overpowering life, death approaches and puts an end to his fufferings.

If after having fafted a length of time, the perfon recover, he becomes melancholy, hyfterical, effeminate, ftupid, &c. †

The functions performed by the fluids and folids of an animal, being fo nearly connected the one with the other, have occafioned this queftion, Does ftarvation operate by inducing difeafe in the folids or fluids ? Moft phyfiologifts are in favour of an opinion, that the fluids are particularly affected, and that by ftarvation the animal fuffers from the quality, rather than from the deficient quantity of the blood. They fuppofe it to become acrid and even putrid.

To determine whether it was the blood that fuffered, I performed the 2d. and 3d. following Experiments, and

alfo

---

* Manchefter Memoirs, Vol. II. p. 575.
† Halleri Elementa Phyfiologiæ.

alfo examined the phænomena prefented by the blood of
an healthy dog, the better to judge of the ftate of that
fluid in all the fucceeding Experiments. And let me here
obferve, that the Experiments I fhall have occafion to relate, were made in the prefence, and with the affiftance of
my ~~many~~ worthy friends, Meffrs. Jeffe Thomfon, John An-
drews my fellow graduate, and Jacob Wagner, junior.
They were witneffes to all the phænomena; and I take
this public method of acknowledging my obligations to
them for their kind affiftance.

EXPERIMENT I.

September 6th. 1792. An ounce of blood was drawn
from one of the crural veins of an healthy dog, at 15 minutes after 2 o'clock, P. M. it was coagulated at 20 minutes after 2; feparation into ferum and craffamentum was
evident at 34 minutes after 2. Serum did not change the
colour of a piece of paper ftained with a vegetable blue. *

EXPERIMENT II.

A young dog was kept for the purpofe of ftarvation,
and the phænomena were as I fhall now relate.

I there-

---

* The vegetable blue was made ufe of as a teft, with the view
of afcertaining whether the ferum of an healthy animal contained any alcaline falt in a formal ftate, as it is a well eftablifhed fact
that the volatile alcali is produced by putrefaction; and the production of it is one of the characteriftic circumftances of that procefs;
the fame teft was made ufe of in the fubfequent experiments, to afcertain whether ferum gained any alcaline properties by the different treatment which the feveral animals fuffered.

I thought it not unneceffary to weigh him, at different times. I fhall therefore mention the weight, as obferved at thofe feveral periods.

July the 8th. he weighed 5¼ lb. July 29th. 7½lb.

Food was given him the laft time, in the afternoon of the 29th. of July.

Auguft 3d. he weighed 6½ lb.

Auguft 12th. he weighed 5lb. At 2 minutes before 12 o'clock an ounce of blood was drawn from one of the crural veffels. The blood flowed freely, but by misfortune an artery was opened inftead of a vein. The colour and fmell of the blood were quite natural, being highly florid like arterial blood. It was coagulated at 3 minutes after 12—feparation into ferum and craffamentum was evident at 13 minutes after 12. The ferum and craffamentum appeared perfectly natural. A piece of the blue ftained paper was dipped into the ferum, and no change of colour was produced. To prevent a further hæmorrhage, as he was much weakened by the bleeding, the wound was well clofed, and a piece of fpunge bound tightly over it. The leg became paralytic.

Auguft 13th. the leg was much fwolen below the ligature, and when handled, did not appear to give him any pain. The ligature was fomewhat loofened.

Auguft 14th. weighed 4½ lb.

Auguft 15th. This morning at 8 o'clock I found him dead.

During

During the above management the dog had very few evacuations by ftool or urine, till the two laft days of his life, when the urine dropped continually from the urethra.

His eyes were feveral times examined, and no alteration in them was evident.

He did not appear to fuffer pain till the 3d. of Auguft, at which time he cried very much, gaped frequently, and appeared very weak; weaknefs continuing daily to in-creafe till his death.

I did not perceive that refpiration was much affected; but the action of the heart became fo feeble, that I could fcarcely perceive its beating for fome days previous to his death, though I applied my hand to the part where its ftroke is generally felt.

The abdomen was much contracted, and the fore-part of it was drawn up to the fpine.

The body was examined immediately on finding him dead, when appearances were as follow:

The ftomach contained a confiderable quantity of a whitifh fluid, its texture was perfectly natural. The in-teftines were of a greenifh caft. The other vifcera ap-peared in a found and natural ftate.

At 39 minutes after 8 o'clock, blood was caught in a tumbler from an opening made into the heart; colour and fmell natural. It was coagulated at 45 minutes after 8. It began to feparate into ferum and craffamentum at 51 minutes after 8. Coagulum and ferum perfectly natural. Serum did not change the paper ftained blue.

EXPE-

EXPERIMENT III.

April 1oth 1793, a dog was kept for the purpofe of *ftarvation.*

April 20th. Blood was drawn from him at 15 minutes paft 3 o'clock. The colour and fmell were natural—it coagulated at 20 minutes after 3—and feparated into ferum and craffamentum at 35 minutes after 3—The ferum was not in the leaft acrid to the tafte.

April 26th. Blood was drawn at 33 minutes paft 3 o'clock—The colour and fmell were natural—It coagulated at 38 minutes paft 3—and feparated into ferum and craffamentum at 53 minutes paft 3—The coagulum and ferum were natural—The ferum was not in the leaft acrid to the tafte.

2dly. *Of Putrid Diet.* The neceffity of our taking aliment being fully eftablifhed, Nature, with her ufual wifdom, has given man and the other animals an appetite for it. She has alfo provided different kinds of aliment in the different climates, in a proper quantity, fo that each might have what was moft fuitable and agreeable to his particular condition.

To this purpofe the appetites of the inhabitants of the different regions vary; while fome prefer a vegetable, others according to the fituation, with more pleafure and benefit to their health, derive their chief fupport from the fame clafs of beings to which they themfelves belong, though of different genera and fpecies.

I

Animals

Animals are ftyled herbivorous, carnivorous, and omni-vorous, from the particular kind of aliment they make ufe of : Thus fheep live wholly on a vegetable diet, while the wolf and other animals of the fame fpecies are found to fupport themfelves beft by a diet which is entirely animal; and man, from the peculiar ftructure of his teeth, appears to be deftined to take in all kinds of alimentary matter, and thus he is found to live beft on a diet, compofed of animal and vegetable fubftances. Experiments would feem to prove that an animal, who is naturally herbivorous, may be made to live entirely on flefh, although not fo conveni-ently. A mixed diet, as already mentioned, beft fuits the appetite and peculiar ftate of man, but there are inftances where he entirely lives on vegetables ; and on the contrary, he has, in other fituations, been found to live wholly on the inferior animals. While the mixed diet renders him placid and fit for every purpofe, for which nature formed him, one entirely animal renders him ferocious as the brute, and that altogether vegetable renders him weak and feeble.

Among civilized nations, aliment, before it is eaten, al-ways undergoes fome kind of preparation, whereby it is rendered more or lefs fit to be fubject of digeftion.

Aliment, after being received into the ftomach, remains there for fome time, and undergoes a confiderable change, before it quits that vifcus ; for it thereby becomes fitted for the forming of the chyle, from which the blood itfelf is immediately prepared.

The ftate of the chyle and confequently that of the blood, is by many fuppofed to be much influenced by the aliment

E   we

we take; thus a putrid and bad diet, is fuppofed to produce vitiated and putrefcent chyle, and. confequently in
their opinion the blood is tainted in the fame manner. This
opinion probably took its rife from the flefh of certain
animals tafting fimilar to the food they eat; thus fea-fowls,
we know, have a fifhy tafte ; pidgeons who have fed on
poke-berries for fometime have their flefh tinged with the
colouring matter of that vegetable ; and the flefh of the
pheafant who has lived upon laurel-berries is capable of
communicating the deadly effects of that active poifon to
the human fyftem. Thefe, and perhaps other like circumftances, were the means of giving rife to the opinion, that
the blood of animals muft be affected differently by different articles of diet, and that corrupted or putrid food
would be the means of producing a putrefaction of the
blood. As long fince as the days of Hippocrates, phyficians have been of opinion that water and corrupted meat
were the true caufes of putrid difeafes. In this manner
was the plague, fcurvy, &c. thought to have been produced; but the fentiment of many moderns is, "That fcurvy
arifes from the want of a due quantity of alimentary matter in the food of thofe who are afflicted with the difeafe." This opinion is fupported by the two cafes of fcurvy related in the Medical Tranfactions by Dr. Milman,
and alfo by Dr. Stark's Dietetic Experiments *.

To convince myfelf whether, the ftate of the blood was
affected by a putrid diet, the following experiments were
performed.

EXPE-

* Vide Blane on Seamen's Difeafes---Medical Tranfactions—and
Stark's Works.

EXPERIMENT IV.

July 29th 1792. A dog was put upon a diet of putrid meat and putrid water, and continued to feed thereon till the 27th day of August following. The meat was beef, and never given to him till it was highly putrid : the drink was clear pump water, rendered putrid by suspending a piece of putrid beef in it, and exposing it to the action of the sun.

August the 12th his eyes were examined, and the pupils of both appeared much contracted. They were watry. At 20 minutes past 12 o'clock an ounce of blood was drawn from one of the crural veins. Its colour and smell were perfectly natural—it was coagulated at 25 minutes after 12— separation into serum and craffamentum was evident at 30 minutes after 12; the coagulum and serum were perfectly natural—the serum did not change the colour of a piece of paper, stained with a vegetable blue.

August 19th. he appears weak and very sick. For these few days past, he has had a disrelish for the putrid meat. His eyes appear sore and inflamed. I washed them with cool pump water. The action of the heart was regular though feeble. Blood was drawn at 4 minutes before 11 o'clock—the colour and smell were perfectly natural— it was coagulated at 11—separation into serum and craffamentum was evident, at 6 minutes after 11. The serum and coagulum were perfectly natural—The serum did not change the colour of the paper stained blue.

August

August 2oth his eyes appear much better—washing them with cold water continued. He appears weak.

August 22d. his eyes appear quite well. Strength some-what recovered. Appetite appears also to be encreased.

August 24th blood was drawn at 20 minutes after 5 o'clock. Its colour and smell were perfectly natural. It was coagulated at 24 minutes after 5—separation into serum and craffamentum was evident at 31 minutes after 5. The coagulum and serum were natural. The serum did not change the colour of the paper stained with the vegeta-blue.

He in general ate and drank a sufficient quantity; but ate more in the beginning than towards the latter end of the experiment. He was reduced by the diet. The ex-cretions were not evidently affected. The action of the heart was regular as has been mentioned, and respiration appeared to be performed in a natural and easy manner.

EXPERIMENT V.

A dog was kept fasting from September the 10th 1792, till the 14th of the same month.

During his fasting he did not appear uneasy till the even-ing of the 13th, when he cried. He continued in this state till the morning of the 14th, when at 15 minutes af-ter 9 o'clock highly putrid broth was given him, he swal-lowed it greedily, belched several times afterwards, but did not vomit. The action of the heart which before was frequent and feeble, now became slower and fuller; he ap-peared

peared very lively and full of play. At 3 o'clock P. M. he was fed again with putrid broth.

September 15th. At 2 o'clock, he received some more of the putrid broth. The action of the heart in every respect natural, except that it was little feeble.

. September 16th. At three o'clock he was fed again with putrid broth which he took in heartily.

September 17th. At 33 minutes after 9 o'clock blood was drawn from one of the crural vessels. Its colour and smell were natural. It was coagulated at 39 minutes after 9. It began to separate into serum and crassamentum at 50 minutes after 9. The serum and coagulum were perfectly natural. The serum had no effect in changing the colour of the paper stained blue.

EXPERIMENT VI.

A bitch was kept under the same circumstances as the dog last mentioned, and the phœnomena were alike in both instances.

September 17th. At 12 minutes before 10 o'clock, blood was drawn. Its colour and smell were natural. It was coagulated at 6 minutes before 10. It began to separate into serum crassamentum at 3 minutes after 10. The serum and coagulum were perfectly natural. The serum did not change the colour of the paper stained blue.

From these experiments, it is evident, that the sensible qualities of the blood are not, in the least, affected by a putrid diet. The question then must certainly be, *How*

does

does a putrid diet operate upon the system? I answer, by inducing debility from the little nourishment it contains ;
and that from hence the solids suffer. This I hope to
prove by an experiment performed on the dog, the sub-
ject of the 19th experiment, which will be related under the
head of injections of putrid matters into the blood-vessels.

The process of *digestion* is one of the most curious ope-
rations of nature. It acts wonderfully and powerfully upon
our aliment, changes the properties of animal and vegetable matters, reduces them both to a substance posses-
sing like properties, and operates upon the hardest as
well as the most fluid substances —All this is said to be
performed by a fluid we call the gastric juice.

If such are the effects of digestion on our aliment, is it
not reasonable to suppose, that the properties of putrid
matters taken into the stomach may be also changed? Let
us examine whether putrid food undergoes a change of
properties in the stomach.

That great Italian Philosopher, Spallanzani, was I be-
live, the first who made experiments to this purpose. He
performed them on birds, cats, dogs, and even went so far
as to swallow putrid meat himself. He found that the
meat, in every instance, lost its putrid smell *.

I repeated his experiments on dogs, with the like suc-
cess, and shall now relate them.

EXPERIMENT VII.

September 17th 1792. Three ounces of highly putrid
beef were given to a bitch. She retained it. Three hours

and

* Spallanzani's Dissertations, Vol. I. p. 284 and seq.

and a half after, the contents of the ſtomach were examined. The meat was found ſurrounded by the gaſtric-fluid ;
its putrid ſmell was entirely deſtroyed, and its colour appeared more natural than it was before the animal had
ſwallowed it.

EXPERIMENT VIII.

September the 17th. 1792. Highly putrid broth was
given to a dog. The ſtomach retained it : and three hours
after, its contents were examined, ſome of the broth was
remaining together with ſome of the ſolid matters that
were mixed with it. The putrid ſmell was found to be
abundantly diminiſhed.

I ſhall now proceed to the conſideration of my 3d.
head, which has for its object of enquiry, Whether the
blood be materially changed and rendered putrid, by the
injection of putrid and other ſubſtances into the bloodveſſels ?

Many centuries have elapſed ſince phyſicians firſt began to be afraid of the acceſs of the leaſt particle of contagious matter into the blood-veſſels, for, that it excited
a fermentation therein, contaminated the whole maſs of
blood, and cauſed it to partake of its contagious properties.

If (ſay they) by adding a ſmall quantity of a ferment to
a maſs of flour, or other fermentable matter, we are able to
bring on a fermentation in it, and convert it into the nature of the ferment, why ſhould not the blood, in like
manner, be affected, if by chance or otherwiſe a putrid

or

or other ferment fhould get into the veffels and mix with it? Thus they fuppofed the fmall-pox, meafles, and other eruptive difeafes to be produced.

Thefe men always overlooked the vital principle, which exifts in the one fubftance, and not in the other; and here in my opinion the material difference lies; for we know that if the other requifite circumftances be duly ob-ferved, it is only neceffary to deftroy life, in order to bring on a putrefaction in the animal. I think, from what I have ftated, there is ground for believing thatt he blood cannot putrefy in the living animal; but the deductions of reafon, however juft and true, the inferences are not to be folely relied upon, when the better evidence of fub-ftantial facts—and of facts more immediately in point than the preceding ones, can be had.

To afcertain beyond a doubt whether the blood could be excited to a putrid fermentation, by injecting putrid matters into the blood-veffels, became an important and ef-fential defideratum. With this view I made the follow-ing Experiments, which were performed *on healthy Dogs.*

The operation of injection was always executed on one or the other of the extremities of the animal. An incifion was made, and the vein was laid bare, which was for fome diftance diffected free from connection with the adjacent parts. An opening was then made into its cavity, fuffici-ciently large to admit a curved tube, which was retained in it by means of a ligature paffed round the veffel. The tube was made fo as to fcrew on the mouth of a common pewter fyringe.

1   E X P E.

EXPERIMENT IX.

Was performed July 29th. 1792, on a Bitch, two months old in good health.

About 5 drachms of putrid ferum were injected into one of her femoral veins. The ferum was obtained from the blood of an healthy dog; and expofed in an open phial, for one week; and had a fmell fimilar to that of rotten eggs.

Some difficulty attended the introduction of the pipe, by which the matter was injected, owing to its large fize, and the fmallnefs of the vein—The vein, when laid bare and touched with any inftrument, contracted confiderably, its diameter being thereby much diminifhed—During the operation, fhe loft but a very inconfiderable quantity of blood, yet fhe feemed very weak and languid, probably owing to the pain fhe endured—Whilft I was injecting the ferum into the vein, fhe had two convulfive paroxyfms, and appeared to be in great pain, which fhe expreffed by feveral loud cries.—The mufcles of her whole body feemed affected with thefe convulfive motions; that they were not owing to the irritation produced by introducing the pipe into the vein is certain, becaufe no fuch fymptoms appeared before the injection of the ferum, though it was introduced twice or thrice.—After the injection was finifhed, fhe was placed on the floor, and attempted to walk, but.was fo weak that fhe fell down. The action of the heart was very frequent, though weak and feeble; refpiration was anxious and difficult. She feemed not at all

inclined

inclined to move, and was quiet, except that at different intervals, she groaned and sighed, and afterwards vomited some of the food she ate at noon, in an indigested state, together with about two ounces of a yellowish green coloured fluid.—Continuing in this situation, she was frequently affected with convulsive motions of the abdominal muscles and lower jaw, she became weaker and weaker. At 15 minutes past 7 o'clock, about an hour and an half after the experiment was performed, all her muscles were in a relaxed state, and she appeared motionless. At half past 7 she was dead.

Dissection. I did not examine the body till the 30th. at half past 8 o'clock; so that she was 13 hours dead, when the examination took place.

The abdomen was much distended; upon cutting into its cavity, a quantity of putrid air, of a smell like that of rotten eggs, rushed out. There was an effusion of a lympid fluid. The intestines were distended with air, and contained but a small quantity of liquid fœces. The stomach contained little else, but a large quantity of the before-mentioned flatus, and a fluid of a yellowish colour. At its lower orifice it appeared rather preternaturally red. All the other viscera were in a found and natural state. The veins appeared much distended; and air, intermixed with with blood, of a dark venous colour, appeared through their coats. When I cut into the vessels, air came out in bubbles, together with the blood. The blood did not appear to be very firmly coagulated. The heart was much distended with blood, particularly the right auricle, which contained some air also.—In the heart the coagulation was more perfect than it was in the veins. The blood did not smell in the least putrid.

EXPE-

EXPERIMENT X.

Was alfo performed July 29th. 1792, on a bitch in good health. About a drachm of pus, diluted with a fmall quantity of clear pump water, was injected into one of her femoral veins. The pus was obtained on the 27th. inft. from an abfcefs of the intercoftal mufcles. This day it poffeffes a putrid fmell.

During the injection of the matter, fhe had two very violent fits of convulfion, the laft of which continued for fome time, and fhe appeared to be in great pain ; refpiration was quick and irregular ; the heart beat frequently, though with fome force. The pulfations were fmall and irregular, accompanied with frequent intermiffions, and to all appearance fhe was dying. When fhe was placed in a cool fituation, the refpiration became lefs difficult, and the action of the heart more regular. She continued in this ftate and lay quiet for fome time, when a mercurial thermometer was applied to the axilla, and the mercury rofe to 100°, as it did when it was applied before fhe underwent the experiment. After lying about twenty minutes in a cool place, fhe got up and attempted to walk, but was very weak, and did not go far before fhe fell down ; after which fhe feemed again to recover. At 30 minutes paft 7 o'clock fhe was feized with twitchings of the mufcles of her abdomen and lower jaw ; the weaknefs encreafed ; at length fhe became motionlefs ; and at 15 minutes before 8 o'clock, about an hour and an half after the injection, fhe was dead.

Diffection.

Diſſection.—The body was not examined till Monday morning the 30th. about 14 hours and an half after ſhe died. The abdomen was conſiderably diſtended, I made an inciſion into it, but found that no air eſcaped—about 2 oz. of a lympid fluid was found effuſed in the cavity. The inteſtines were much diſtended, and when an inciſion was made into them, air and fæces come out. The ſtomach was likewiſe much diſtended with air and half digeſted food. The ſame preternatural redneſs about the lower orifice, which occurred in the former caſe, appeared alſo in this. The other abdominal viſcera appeared perfectly natural and found The heart was much diſtended with blood, but no air was found in it or the blood-veſſels. The blood was more firmly coagulated than that mentioned in the laſt Experiment, and it had no unnatural ſmell.

EXPERIMENT XI.

Auguſt 6th. 1792. A drachm of fluid matter, produced by highly putrid beef, was diluted with four drachms of putrid pump water, and injected into one of the femoral veins of an healthy dog.

The matter was injected at half an hour after 11 o'clock. During the injection he was much convulſed, and appeared to be in great pain. The pupils of the eyes were ſomewhat dilated. The beating of the heart was now very frequent, though feeble, as it was during the injection of the matter. At 15 minutes before 12 o'clock the breathing became very frequent, accompanied with great difficulty and ſighing. At this time he vomit-

ed

ed a quantity of half digefted food, and appeared to be greatly relieved by it; at 12 o'clock he vomited again, which relieved him fo that he rofe, but in one or two minutes laid down again. At 4 minutes paft 12 he had an evacuation of fæces—at 7 minutes after 12 he attempted to lay down, but fell, and laid in an unnatural pofture—he appeared to be very weak—his breathing became more difficult and laborious—his eyes appeared watry and funk in the orbits. At 10 minutes paft 12 he had another evacuation of fæces. At 15 minutes after 12 he was raifed up on his feet—he ftood, though with difficulty, and his left hind leg became paralytic *. In a fhort time all his hind parts appeared to be more or lefs affected in this manner. At 40 minutes after 12 he became very reftlefs, turning and twifting his body every way. At 45 minutes after 12 he was again raifed upon his feet, but could not ftand, for all his mufcles appeared greatly relaxed. At 1 o'clock the pupils of his eyes were much dilated, and his fight feemed to be greatly diminifhed—he had an evacuation of urine. He began to groan, and the abdominal mufcles were convulfed. The convulfions, after continuing fome time in thofe parts, extended to the mufcles of his head and neck. Refpiration, and the action of the heart ceafing, he died at 12 minutes paft 10 o'clock.

Diffection. The body was examined immediately after death, and nothing unufual was obferved. The blood was quite natural in every refpect.

E X P E-

---

* The incifion in this Experiment was made on the *right* thigh.

Auguſt 10th. 1792. Twelve grains of putrid blood, diluted with a drachm of clear pump water, were in-jeĉted into one of the femoral veins of an healthy bitch, at thirty-five minutes paſt 10 o'clock. During the injeĉtion ſhe ſeemed uneaſy, and had an evacuation of urine. The aĉtion of the heart became much ſlower, and very feeble. Reſpiration was ſomewhat difficult. She was then placed on the floor, and continued ſtanding —12 minutes after ſhe had a natural motion from the reĉtum, and then laid down. At 11 o'clock her eyes were examined, and they did not appear any way preter-natural. She ſeemed dull, heavy, and much inclined to ſleep. At 12 o'clock I perceived that ſhe had had ano-ther evacuation of urine. The eyes were now examined again, and no alteration appeared to have taken place in them. She laid quiet till half paſt 1 o'clock, when vio-lent efforts to vomit came on, and ſhe brought up a quantity of the food ſhe had eaten previouſly to the per-forming of the experiment. The heart beat very fre-quent and feeble—reſpiration was not greatly affeĉted, but ſhe continued dull and heavy. At 2 o'clock meat and drink were offered her—ſhe would not even bear the ſmell of meat, but roſe and drank ſome water. She laid down. At half paſt 2 o'clock ſhe got up again, walked about, and evacuated urine; then laid down again, and was dull and heavy as before. At 5 minutes before 5 o'clock ſhe had another evacuation of urine. At 3 mi-nutes before 5 ſhe had a very copious evacuation of ex-tremely fluid fæces, of the colour of coffee-grounds, and of a very putrid ſmell. She now appeared weaker than

ſhe

she was before the evacuation, though not quite so dull.
At 6 o'clock she evacuated urine again. I left her at 25
minutes after 6, when circumstances did not appear much
altered. At 8 o'clock I saw her again, meat and drink
were offered her—she drank, but would not eat. The
heart beat very frequent and feeble—in other respects as
before.

August 11th. This morning, at 8 o'clock, I found her
dead. A disagreeable odour arose from her body. The
abdomen appeared somewhat distended. I perceived she
had had another loose evacuation of the description above
mentioned, though not so copious as the former one.
There was a great deal of saliva about the mouth, and
the tongue protruded through the teeth. On

Dissection, the following appearances were observed.
Upon cutting into the cavity of the abdomen, no air es-
caped, but I experienced a very disagreeable foetid smell.
The superior parts of the intestines appeared in several
places of a dark green colour, spotted with small white
specks, while the lower portions appeared natural.
When an incision was made into the intestines, a quantity
of putrid air rushed out, together with liquid dark green
coloured fæces. The stomach appeared to be rather
small—I made an incision into it when some of the like
liquor flowed out. The liver was in many places of a
preternatural colour, and adhered to almost all the other
abdominal viscera, particularly to the stomach and right
kidney. The gall-bladder was much distended with a
light green coloured bile; the lungs were collapsed; the
right lobes were of a blackish colour, intermixed with
red; the left lobes appeared natural. The red appearance

ance at the lower orifice of the ſtomack, mentioned in the other caſes, was not apparent in this. The veins and heart were much diſtended with blood, which was not very firmly coagulated, but its ſmell was perfectly natural.

EXPERIMENT XIII.

Auguſt 14th, 1792. At 40 minutes after 10 o'clock ſix grains of putrid blood, mixed with a drachm and an half of clear pump water, were injected into one of the femoral veins of a bitch. During the injection ſhe appeared very uneaſy—the action of the heart was ſlow and feeble—reſpiration ſlow, and performed with difficulty. She was placed on the floor, appeared dull, and laid down. At 10 minutes before 11 o'clock her abdominal muſcles were violently convulſed. At 7 minutes before 11 ſhe was ſeized with violent retchings and efforts to vomit, but did not evacuate. At 15 minutes before 3 o'clock meat and drink were offered her—ſhe ate, but would not drink. At 23 minutes before 7 ſhe had a copious evacuation of urine. At 20 minutes before 7 ſhe ate and drank. I left her at 15 minutes before 7, when ſhe ſeemed eaſy. I ſaw her again at 8 o'clock and no alteration was evevident.

Auguſt 15th. This morning, at 8 o'clock, I ſaw her— ſhe appeared perfectly eaſy—action of the heart nearly natural, though rather frequent. She was now fed, and ate as before. I perceived that ſhe had had a natural evacuation of fæces. At 21 minutes after 5 blood was drawn—its colour and ſmell were natural—it was coagulated at 24 minutes after 5—the ſeparation into ſerum and

craſſamentum

craffamentum was evident at 30 minutes after 5—a piece of the paper ftained blue was dipped into the ferum, and no change of colour took place—the ferum and coagulum were quite natural. I faw her again at 8 o'clock. She appeared as fhe did when in health.

Auguft 16th. She was perfectly well.

EXPERIMENT XIV.

Auguft 17th. 1792. At 15 minutes after 12 o'clock twelve grains of putrid blood, mixed with a drachm and an half of clear pump water, were injected into one of the humeral veins of the bitch laft mentioned. During the injec-tion, fhe cried violently, and appeared to be in great pain. Refpiration became very frequent—action of the heart frequent and feeble. The eyes were examined, and the pupils were found to be much contracted. She was placed on the floor, walked a few fteps, leaned againft the wall, in a ftanding pofture, and appeared very fick. At 26 minutes after 12 fhe had an evacuation of fæces, which was rather loofe. At half paft 12 fhe laid down, appeared dull, and much inclined to fleep. At half paft 2 the abdominal mufcles were affected with convulfive contractions—they did not continue long. The eyes were again examined, and the pupils appeared natural. At 3 minutes before 5 fhe had a copious evacuation of urine. At 10 minutes after 6 I left her eating, and to appearance eafy, though dull and languid. I faw her again at 8 o'clock, when I perceived fhe had had another loofe evacuation of fæces, which was copious. Pulfation of the heart frequent and feeble—fhe appeared eafy.

G

Auguft

August 18th. Blood was drawn at 5 minutes before
6 o'clock P. M.—its colour and fmell were natural
—it was coagulated at 6—at 5 five minutes after 6 it
feparated into ferum and craffamentum—coagulum and
ferum were quite natural—Serum did not change the paper ftained blue. At 8 fhe appeared perfectly well.

August 19th. She was perfectly well. The blood,
which was drawn yefterday, had a natural odour, when
it was examined this morning at 11 o'clock.

EXPERIMENT XV.

August 20th. 1792. At 4 minutes before 11 o'clock,
half a drachm of putrid blood and a drachm of clear pump-
water, were injected into one of the humoral veins of the
laft mentioned bitch during the injection, fhe was very uneafy and gave feveral loud fhrieks. The heart beat very
frequent and feeble. Refpiration became very difficult.
She was placed on the floor, and immmediately after
had a copious evacuation from the ftomach. She appeared very weak, and leaned againft the wall. At 7
minutes after 11, fhe had retchings and violent efforts
to vomit, but no evacuation enfued. At 32 minutes after
11, fhe began to groan and figh. At five minutes after 12, fhe had efforts to vomit, but nothing was thrown
up. I left her at 15 minutes before 1; fhe drank, and
appeared eafy, though fhe was very weak. I faw her again
at 2 o'clock, the heart beat very frequent and feeble. I
perceived fhe had had an evacuation of fæces, while I was
abfent—it was rather loofe. Meat and drink were offered
her; fhe drank, but did not eat. She appeared very fick.

I faw

. I faw her again at 8'clock, when fhe appeared juft as fhe was at 2 o'clock.

Auguft 21ft. Blood was drawn at 2 minutes before 5 o'clock P. M. its colour and fmell were natural—it was coagulated at 3 minutes after 5—feparation into ferum and craffamentum was evident at 9 minutes after 5 —the coagulum and ferum were perfectly natural—the ferum did not change the color of the paper ftained blue. At 8 o'clock fhe appeared very well.

Auguft 22d. Serum of the blood drawn yefterday, did not change the colour of the paper ftained blue.

EXPERIMENT XVI.

Auguft 22d. 1792. At 11 o'clock, a drachm of putrid blood mixed with half a drachm of clear pump water, was injected into one of the crural veins of the bitch laft mentioned. During the injection, the action of the heart became very frequent and feeble. Refpiration very laborious. She vomited. After this fhe was placed on the floor, and appeared very weak, yet ftood for fome minutes, and then fell down gently. At 8 minutes after 11, fhe had an evacuation of urine and of fæces. At 14 minutes after 11, the eyes were examined; the pupils were found to be very much contracted, and her fight much diminifhed. At 16 minutes after 11, fhe had another evacuation of urine. At 19 minutes after 11, fhe began to cry violently, and appeared to be in very great pain. The refpiration became very laborious, and the action of the heart encreafed in frequency and feeblenefs. At 23 minutes af-

ter

ter 11, fhe became convulfed. At 25 minutes after 11, a finger was drawn over the eye, and no contraction of the eye-lids took place. At 28 minutes after 11, fhe was dead.

Diffection. The examination of the body took place at 8 minutes after 12 o'clock. All the vifcera were found in a found and natural ftate, except the lungs—there a bloody effufion was difcovered, particularly in the inferior parts of the left lobes. At 20 minutes after 12, blood was obtained by opening one of the large veins; the colour and fmell were natural. When I left the blood, it was not fo perfectly coagulated, as in the other inftances, owing to its having been by accident much agitated. I returned in the afternoon, and found the coagulation complete—the coagulum and ferum were natural—the ferum did not change a piece of paper ftained blue.

EXPERIMENT XVII.

Auguft 14th. 1792. At 16 minutes after 3 o'clock, fix grains of putrid blood, diluted with a drachm of clear pump water, were injected into one of the femoral veins of an healthy dog. During the injection, he was very uneafy and gave feveral loud fhrieks. The action of the heart became fo feeble, that it could fcarcely be felt, and was alfo frequent. He was placed on the floor, when he lay down. In a fhort time he rofe up, ftood fometime, and appeared very weak. Refpiration became laborious, and he lay down again. At 15 minutes before 4 o'clock, he was feized with twitchings about the botttom of, and acrofs the thorax, in a great degree refembling an hiccup.

At

At 4 minutes after 4, meat and drink were offered him; he would not drink, and seemed as if defirous to eat; but when he approached near the meat, he drew his head from it, as if the fmell of it were offenfive to him, though the meat was frefh killed this morning. At 2 minutes before 5, he had an evacuation of urine, and rather a loofe evacuation from the rectum. At 4 minutes after 5 he had a copious evacuation from the ftomach, when the action of the heart became perceptible to the touch. At 20 minutes after 5, he had violent efforts to vomit, and brought up a quantity of greenifh coloured fluid. At 34 minutes after 5, they recurred again, with the like effect. They attacked him a third time at 3 minutes before 6; the confequence was the fame as in both the former inftances. I left him at 15 minutes before 7 o'clock; when he was eating and drinking. He feemed eafy.

I faw him again at 8 o'clock, when he appeared heavy. I perceived that fince I had left him, he had had a fparing evacuation of fæces, rather loofe.

Auguft 15th. This morning at 8 o'clock, he appeared dull, heavy and weak. The action of the heart was frequent and feeble. He was now fed. At 2 o'clock, I faw him again; he was as defcribed in the morning.

At 5 o'clock, blood was drawn—the colour and fmell were natural—it coagulated at 4 minutes after 5—feparation into ferum and craffamentum took place, at 12 minutes after 5—the colour of the paper ftained blue was not changed by the ferum—The coagulum and ferum were
perfectly

perfectly natural—I faw him again at 8 o'clock, and he appeared perfectly well.

August 16th. He was perfectly well to-day.

EXPERIMENT XVIII.

August 17th. 1792. At 15 minutes after 4 o'clock, ten grains of putrid blood, mixed with a drachm of clear pump water, were injected into one of the femoral veins of the dog laft mentioned. During the injection, he appeared to be in much pain, and had an evacuation of urine; the action of the heart became frequent and feeble, but refpiration was not much altered. At half paft 4, the abdominal mufcles were convulfed; the convulfions did not laft any length of time. At 20 minutes before 5, he was feized with tremors over his whole body; they lafted about two minutes, and then went off. At 16 minutes before 5, he had an evacuation of urine. At 15 minutes after 6, I left him eating, when he appeared pretty eafy. I faw him again at 8 o'clock, and perceived he had had a motion fince I left him. The action of the heart was frequent and feeble. While I was with him he had an eva- cuation of urine, and appeared eafy.

August 18th. Blood was drawn at 10 minutes after 6 o'clock this morning—its colour and fmell were natural —it was coagulated at 14 minutes after 6—feparation in- to ferum and craffamentum began to take place at 23 mi- nutes after 6. The coagulum and ferum were natural. The ferum did not change the colour of the paper ftained blue. At 8 he appeared to be perfectly well.

August

Auguſt 19th. He was perfectly well to-day. The blood, that was drawn yeſterday, was examined this morning, and poſſeſſed no unnatural ſmell.

EXPERIMENT XIX.

Auguſt 27th. 1792. At 40 minutes before 10 o'clock, a drachm of putrid blood, mixed with half a drachm of clear pump-water was injected into one of the femoral veins of the dog, the ſubject of the 4th. Experiment. During the injection, he was very uneaſy, and evacuated urine. The action of the heart became very frequent and feeble. He was placed on the floor, and immediately after vomited. At 3 minutes before 10, he had an evacuation of natural fæces. At 2 minutes before 10, he vomited again. At 10 his breathing became very laborious, and he had a looſe and ſmall evacuation of natural coloured fæces. At 3 minutes after 10, he lay down. The heart beat ſo feeble, that it could ſcarcely be felt. At 10 minutes after 10, he roſe, vomited again, and then lay down. At 15 minutes after 10, the eyes were examined and no alteration in them was apparent. At 21 minutes after 10, he roſe again, walked about the room, ſtood for ſometime, and then again lay down. The action of the heart became more evident. At 11 o'clock, he groaned very much. At 6 minutes after 11 the action of the heart became more frequent and feeble. The eyes were now again examined, but preſented no unnatural appearance. At 20 minutes after 11, he roſe and walked a few ſteps, had a ſparing evacuation of chocolate-coloured, liquid fæces, then fell down, and appeared as if ſtimulated to evacuate again; he roſe and had an evacuation of urine, and again fell down. At 18 minutes before 12, his abdominal

dominal mufcles became convulfed. At 4 minutes before
12, he vomited again. At 28 minutes after 12, he rofe,
walked a few fteps, had an evacuation of very thin chocolate-coloured fæces, and appeared to be very weak; after
this he walked a few fteps again, and then lay down. I
left him at 10 minutes before 1 o'clock, when he appeared eafy, though very weak and fick. When I returned,
at 12 minutes before 3, I perceived, that during my ab-
fence, he had had two or three evacuations of urine. The
heart beat frequently and feebly. At 10 minutes before
3, he had an evacuation of urine, and afterwards vomited. At 8 minutes before three, he had an evacuation of
very liquid fæces, intermixed with mucus. At 5 minutes before 3, he had retchings and efforts to vomit, but did not
evacuate. At 16 minutes before three, he rofe, and had
another evacuation of fæces fimilar to the one laft mentioned. At 10 minutes after 4, he had an evacuation
from the rectum, of mucus intermixed with blood. At
25 minutes after 4, putrid meat and putrid water were offered him, he drank plentifully, but did not eat. I left
him at half paft 4, and faw him again at half paft 7, when
I perceived he had had a very copious evacuation of urine,
but had not eaten. The heart beat frequently, though
not fo feebly as before. Refpiration was pretty free. He
feemed eafy, and appeared much better than when I left
him the laft time.

August 28th. When I faw him this morning at 8
o'clock, marks of an evacuation of fæces and urine were
evident. I perceived he had eaten nothing. Putrid water was given him and he drank of it. The heart beat
frequently and feebly. He appeared very weak; and the

wound put on a bad appearance. At 2 o'clock I faw him again, when I perceived that he had had two or three evacuations of urine, but that he had not eaten. I now offered him fome frefh meat, he held it in his mouth, but did not fwallow any of it, and let it drop. Putrid water was again offered to him and he drank it. Refpiration did not appear to be much affected. The action of the heart was frequent; and fo feeble as fcarcely to be felt. In my prefence he had an evacuation of urine; I caught fome of it in an earthen veffel, dipped a piece of the blue-coloured paper in it, but no change of the colour was evident. The wound appeared in a gangrenous ftate. He feemed very weak, and it was with difficulty that he ftood. At 8 minutes before 5; blood was drawn; the colour and fmell were natural. It coagulated at 4 minutes before 5; feparation into ferum and craffamentum was evident, at 7 minutes after 5; the ferum and craffinentum were perfectly natural; the ferum did not change the colour of the paper ftained blue. The wound appeared much worfe. In every other cafe, yet mentioned, it invariably put on a good appearancee, and healed readily. After bleeding he appeared exceedingly weak. At 35 minutes after 5, I left him very uncafy. I faw him again at 8 o'clock, and he appeared nearly in the fame condition as when I left him laft.

Auguft 29th. This morning at 8 o'clock, I found him dead. The blood drawn yefterday, was now examined. No unnatural fmell was evident. The ferum did not change the colour of the paper ftained blue. The coagulum was fo firm, that when thrown out of the tumbler on the floor, it did not break. A very difagreeable and fœtid odour arofe from the body.

H   *Diffec-*

Diffection. The body was examined at half paſt 9 o'clock, when I cut through the ſkin covering the lower ribs, the fleſh below appeared gangrenous. The liver in ſome places was of rather a lighter colour than natural. The inferior part of the ſmall inteſtines appeared inflamed. The ſtomach was perfectly natural, both internally and externally; it contained mucus and a whitiſh fluid. A bloody effuſion was found in the lungs, particularly in the right lobes. The bladder was quite natural. The heart and veins were much diſtended with blood, which was firmly coagulated in both; the colour and ſmell of it were perfectly natural.

As yeaſt is well known to be a powerful ferment, and the volatile alcali a great chemical agent, and a diſſolver of the blood when out of the body, the following Experiments were made, to aſcertain what effect they would have on the blood, when injected into the blood-veſſels.

EXPERIMENT XX.

Auguſt 14th. 1792. At 20 minutes after 11 o'olock three drachms of ſtock-yeaſt were injected into one of the femoral veins of a dog. During the injection he appeared ſomewhat uneaſy. Reſpiration became very difficult and laborious; the action of the heart irregular, intermitting, and ſomewhat encreaſed in force. He was placed on the floor but was not able to ſtand. At 30 minutes after 11, he had an evacuation of urine; at 33 minutes after 11, he had an evacuation of natural fæces. The eyes being examined, did not appear evidently altered. The muſcles of his whole body now ſeemed to be in a relaxed

laxed ftate. At 40 minutes after 11, his eye-fight appeared to be much diminifhed ; at 5 minutes before 12, he was dead.

Diffeƈtion. The body was examined immediately after death. Nothing preternatural was obferved, except a bloody effufion in the lungs. The blood was in every refpeƈt natural.

EXPERIMENT XXI.

Auguft 7th. 1792. At 20 minutes before 11 o'clock, 15 grains of mild volatile alcali diffolved in two drachms of clear pump water, were injeƈted into one of the femoral veins of an healthy bitch. During the injeƈtion, fhe gave three or four loud cries, and feemed to be in great pain. She was placed on the floor, walked three or four fteps, and then lay down. The aƈtion of the heart was encreafed in frequency, and refpiration was performed with difficulty. In other refpeƈts fhe feemed eafy and quiet. At 11 o'clock, meat and drink were offered to her; fhe would not take of either. Refpiration now feemed to be performed with no great difficulty. The aƈtion of the heart was as before mentioned. At 35 minutes paft 4, the eyes were examined, and they appeared no ways altered. At 42 minutes paft 11, fhe began to be reftlefs. The aƈtion of the heart feemed to have recovered fome degree of quicknefs ; the frequency of it ftill continued. Refpiration appeared pretty eafy, though fhort. At 40 minutes paft 12, her whole body was feized with a tremulous motion, when a thermometer was applied to the axilla, and the temperature was as when in health. Thefe tremors came on in paroxyfms, each of which lafted but a little time, and they recurred frequently. The heart, during a paroxyfm of trembling, beat frequently and feebly. The tremors encreafed in violence, and in frequency of recurrence. At 14 minutes paft 1, fhe was affected with feveral violent convulfive contractions acrofs her abdomen. At half paft 1, the eyes were again examined, and the pupils were obferved alternately to dilate and contract frequently and confiderably. At 40 minutes after 1, fhe rofe, looked about; meat and drink were again offered her, but fhe refufed both, and lay down again. At 10 minutes before 2, the tremors attacked her again, her breathing became more difficult and laborious, the tremors continued more or lefs violent for 5 minutes, then went off, and fhe appeared eafy. At 15 minutes after 2, the tremors and laborious breathing came on again; they were of fhort duration; when they went off fhe appeared eafy, and continued fo till 5 minutes after 4, when they occurred again. At 10 minutes after 4, fhe gave three or four loud cries, as if affected with much pain, then was eafy again, and remained fo till 40 minutes after 5, when I left her. At 8 o'clock I faw her again; fhe feemed perfectly eafy, the action of the heart was frequent and feeble.

Auguft 8th. At 8 o'clock this morning fhe appeared eafy, but was very weak; and her heart beat frequently and feebly. She now ate and drank; at 2 o'clock fhe appeared as in the morning: I alfo perceived that fhe had had a natural evacuation from the rectum fince I faw her in the morning, which was the firft that occurred fince the operation was performed. At 7 o'clock I faw her again; no alteration was evident. I found that fhe had had a natural evacuation of fæces this afternoon; but I did not perceive any marks of a difcharge of urine.

Auguft

Auguſt 9th. She ſeemed quite well, but drank more than dogs uſually do in health.

EXPERIMENT XXII.

Auguſt 10th. 1792. At 40 minutes after 11 o'clock, 25 grains of mild volatile alcali, diſſolved in two drachms of clear pump-water were injeċted into the bitch laſt mentioned. During the injeċtion, ſhe was violently con-vulſed, and gave ſeveral loud cries ; ſhe alſo had an evacu-ation of urine and vomited. The heart beat very fre-quently, and breathing was laborious. She was placed on the floor, ran about the room, and then lay down. Her aſpeċt was very wild. She did not lay long before ſhe got up again ; but in a few minutes lay down. At half paſt one ſhe roſe, and immediately afterwards lay down a-gain. The breathing was very frequent. At 2, meat and drink were offered her, but ſhe did not take of either. I left her at 25 minutes after 6, ſhe continuing to be in the ſame condition. At 8 o'clock I ſaw her again ; meat and drink were then offered her, ſhe drank, but would not eat. Her heart beat very frequently, though weak ; ſhe ſeemed in other reſpeċts as ſhe was before.

Auguſt 11th. This morning at 8 o'clock ſhe appeared to be eaſy, was quiet, and ate and drank. Her heart beat frequently and feebly. I ſaw her again at 8 in the evening; ſhe was in the ſame condition as in the morning. At 26 mi-nutes after 8 blood was drawn—its colour and ſmell were quite natural—it coagulated at 32 minutes after 8 o'clock—ſeparation into ſerum and craſſamentum was evident at 38

minutes

minutes after 8 o'clock—the coagulum and ferum were every way natural—the ferum did not change the colour of the paper ftained blue.

Auguft 12th. To-day fhe appeared perfectly well.

EXPE·RIMENT XXIII.

Auguft 13th. 1792. At 15 minutes before 11 o'clock 45 grains of mild volatile alcali diffolved in two drachms and an half of clear pump water, were injected into the fame bitch. During the injection fhe appeared to be in great pain, and gave feveral loud cries. She was placed on the floor, ran about the room, then lay down, and was very reftlefs. The action of the heart was extremely frequent, and her afpect was wild. After lying a few minutes fhe became eafy. At 35 minutes after 2 meat and drink were offered her; fhe ate, but would not drink. At 30 minutes after 4 o'clock blood was drawn—its colour and fmell were natural—it coagulated at 35 minutes after 4—feparation into ferum and craffamentum was evident at 39 minutes after 4—the craffamentum and ferum were perfectly natural—the ferum did not change the colour of the paper ftained blue. At 39 minutes after 4 more blood was drawn from the fame vein—its colour and fmell were natural: As foon as it was drawn, I added 45 grains of mild volatile alcali diffolved in ʒij of clear pump water to it, when the colour became a very deep brown, nearly black. At 8 minutes before 5 o'clock it appeared to have a tendency to coagulate. At 10 minutes before 6 it was of the confiftence of mucus. At 10 minutes after 6 fhe feemed perfectly eafy, and was eating meat. At 8 o'clock fhe appeared in the fame eafy fituation.

Auguft

Auguſt 14th. At 8 o'clock this morning ſhe appeared perfectly eaſy. The blood laſt mentioned was examined, and its conſiſtence was much as before.

From the above Experiments the following Inferences reſult:

1ſt. That, contrary to the generally received opinion, the blood is neither rendered alcaline, acrid or putrid by ſtarvation. This I think is evinced by theſe circumſtances—that the blood went through its ſpontaneous changes in the regular and uſual manner—that the ſerum had no effect in changing the colour of my teſt—and that no ſenſe of acrimony was perceptible to the taſte.

2dly. That a Putrid Diet does not operate upon the blood ſo as to change its ſenſible properties. This is a material part of the enquiry, ſince phyſicians, from Hippocrates down to the preſent day, have ſuppoſed various and wonderful changes to be produced in the animal œconomy by ſuch food. From the above Experiments, it appears very clear, that a putrid diet had no effect whatever in changing the qualities of the blood, although the animals were ſtrictly confined to it. We are alſo led to conclude from them, that a putrid diet does not change the ſenſible qualities of the excretions; ſince, as I have related, the urine did not alter the colour of the vegetable blue. Here it may be objected to me, that I ought merely to infer from theſe Experiments, that the blood of dogs only is not affected by this treatment—I anſwer, that the inference may, probably, be extended to the whole animal creation; for, we cannot but ſuppoſe that nature is, in this reſpect, as beneficent to the one ſpecies as ſhe is to the

other;

other; and to substantiate this opinion, I avail myself of the result of the Experiments of the celebrated Spallanzani as above mentioned, who not only operated upon the brute creation, but went so far as to risk his own life for the benefit of science; and found, contrary to the received opinion, that vitiated food, previous to its leaving the stomach, is converted into a matter capable of furnishnishing good blood. "Men, such as the inhabitants about the mouth of the Orange river, in Africa, live always on animal food, such as whales, seals, limpets, and what fish they can catch; that many times their food has entered into a great degree of putrefaction, and there is no vegetable food whatever employed at the same time; probably most of them never tasted any vegetable substance in their lives, excepting aromatics for seasoning; yet they are perfectly healthy and free from all putrefaction in their fluids or solids, though they are not very careful of avoiding it in the exterior parts of the body. We see likewise maggots live in and upon putrid masses, while they themselves, and all their fluids, are perfectly sweet and free from all appearance of putrefaction*." There appears to be an intimate connection between the fluid and solid parts of our bodies, but how far this connection between them subsists, I will not undertake to assert. Perhaps I might, in truth, have said that a putrid diet acts upon the solids of our machine, by its not containing alimentary matter in a proper quantity, and therefore not affording a sufficiency of blood to support the animal. We know that the solids derive their nourishment from the blood; and, in my opinion, it is sufficiently evidenced, from the mortification of the muscular parts which ensued upon making an incision into the thigh, as

has

* Fordyce on Digestion, p. 155.

has been already ftated—That a putrid diet does operate upon the folids.

3dly. That although the blood, or other animal, matter may be excited into a putrid fermentation out of the body, by the addition of a putrid ferment, yet that fuch a procefs cannot be excited in the living body. We have found that many grains of putrid matter exifted in the blood-veffels for fome days without changing the blood. Is it probable that a fermentation can be induced in the blood when the ferment enters the fyftem by abforption, and no fuch procefs take place by introducing a putrid ferment immediately into the blood-veffels?

4thly. That by the introduction of putrid matter into the blood-veffels, very violent fymptoms were produced, although the quantity of the matter was fmall, and of the fame nature as the blood, except that it had become putrid*. Is it probable, then, that the animal could exift with the whole mafs of blood in a ftate of putrefaction, when fuch violent fymptoms were the confequence of the introduction of fo fmall a quantity of putrid matter as was injected in the foregoing Experiments?

And, 5thly. That though the volatile alcali may operate upon the blood in a wonderful manner out of the body, it does not evidently affect the blood when injected into the blood-veffels.

I   From

* My reafon for making ufe of putrid ferum and putrid blood, is, that they are the fame fubftance, only altered by putrefaction. We know, from Experiments of Transfufion, that blood may be paffed from the veffels of one animal, into thofe of another, without any evident injury. From this circumftance we are led to infer, that it, in thefe inftances, acted as putrid matter.

From thefe experiments it is alfo evident, that cathartic and emetic medicines, when injected into the blood-vef-fels, cannot operate in a fpecific manner ; for in almoft every inftance evacuations were the confequence of the ex-periments when neither cathartics nor emetics were inject-ed. Probably any matter capable of producing a fufficient irritation, will produce thofe effects, when thus thrown into the animal.

I attribute the prefence of air in the veffels and heart, which occurred in one of the experiments, to the imper-fect ftate of the fyringe ; for it confifted of one whole piece, when the two firft experiments were performed.

Before I leave this part of the enquiry, I beg leave to ftate the following queftions, viz.

Is there a power in the blood-veffels, or in the blood, capable of affimilating to the blood matters which are in-jected into the veffels ? Do not the following circumftan-ces make it probable ? I could not by a minute examina-tion diftinguifh between the blood and the matter injected. The ferum of the blood, where the volatile alkali was in-jected did not poffefs the odour of that falt, neither did it change the colour of the paper ftained with a vegetable blue. Does not the doctrine of fecretion, which is now gaining ground, favour fuch an idea ? I own that there are certain exceptions to this opinion.

Do not the lofs of vifion, the dilated and contracted pupil, together with the convulfions which happened, denote the nervous fyftem to be affected by the contents of the blood-veffels ?

I fhall

I fhall now proceed to enquire, whether there is any reafon to believe that the blood becomes putrid in any difeafe ?

This is a queftion of confiderable importance. Extenfive experience is neceffary to decide it; and as my own has been very limited with regard to difeafes fuppofed to be putrid, I muft beg leave to refer the unprejudiced reader to books, which treat at large of them. Perhaps upon thorough confideration, he will believe the matter to be at leaft doubtful.

All I can do, will be to ftate fome objections to the inferences that have been drawn from the fymptoms and circumftances attending thefe difeafes.

A fymptom on which great ftrefs has been laid, is, the appearance of Petechiæ, Vibices, or effufions of blood, which takes place in the laft ftage of Typhus, Yellow Fever, Scurvy &c. Thefe appearances are generally fuppofed to be indicative of a diffolved ftate of the blood, in thofe difeafes, though in my opinion without a fufficient reafon. It is conceded by all that the fyftem in thofe difeafes is very much debilitated, and of confequence the fyftem of bloodveffels, and thefe particularly at their ultimate terminations. The effect of this debility is a relaxation of the folids; the fibres of the blood-veffels will not now be in as clofe contact as they were in health, and the mouths of the exhalents will not be as narrowly contracted. This particular ftate of the veffels at their terminations, will allow the blood to tranfude, and be effufed in the cellular membrane; or the exhalents, which in health pour out a lympid fluid, may now be capable of forwarding the

red

red blood itſelf. Analogy ſupports the opinion. Do not the veſſels of the eye in ophthalmia, through which a colourleſs lymph is circulated in health, receive in this diſeaſed ſtate, red globules? Do we not find in dropſy, that the veſſels allow of a greater exhalation than when in health? If in proportion as we become debilitated, we approach nearer to a ſtate of death, Does not the tranſudation of bile through the coats of the gall-bladder, in dead ſubjects, give additional ſtrength to the idea? Again, is it not confirmed by the circumſtance, that theſe appearances take place in the laſt ſtage of thoſe diſeaſes when the debility is greateſt?

If Petechiæ were true ſymptoms of a diſſolved and putrid ſtate of the blood, we ſhould certainly find that the bodies of thoſe who die, marked with ſuch ſymptoms, would certainly putrefy much ſooner than the bodies of others who die without any ſuch marks. The contrary of this is ſaid to happen: And anatomiſts aſſert " that the bodies of thoſe who die, of what are called putrid fevers, are longer before they undergo real putrefaction than of thoſe who die of other diſeaſes, or who die in perfect health by violence." *

The diſſections of the celebrated Lind and Rouppe, ſeem to prove that the blood in thoſe diſeaſes is not putrid. The former found it in the yellow-fever to be grumous and viſcid, and covered with a yellow gluten, impenetrable to the finger unleſs cut by the nail †

The

* Moore's Medical Sketches.
† Lind's firſt paper on Fevers and Infection, p. 13. & ſeq.

The fame gentleman relates; " that in fcurvy, red coagulated blood is found extravafated in almoſt all parts of the body, not only into the tela cellulofa, but into the bellies of the mufcles, particularly of the legs and thighs, which often become quite ſtuffed, and even diſtorted, with large grumous maſſes *."

After ſtating that, " Some authors from a fuppofition of the great diſſolution of the blood in petechial fevers, and from another fuppofition, that bliſters encreaſed the d'ſſolution of that fluid ſtill more, have forbid their application in fuch fevers." He adds, " But the experience of the moſt eminent practitioners does not fupport thoſe theoretical opinions †."

Rouppe, a phyfician who had great experience in the fcurvy, found that the blood was always more or leſs coagulated in thoſe inſtances, in which he had an opportunity of viewing it. He obferves, " If we confider, we fhall find that the blood of thoſe who have a continual fever, or an inflammation, after they have loſt a good deal by bleeding, is fo diſſolved, that no one can find blood of a thinner confiſtency even in the laſt ſtage of the fcurvy. Who (he juſtly interrogates) has even pretended to fay theſe difeaſes were owing to a diſſolved or putrid ſtate of the blood ‡?"

We may further obferve, that a diſſolved ſtate of the blood is by no means a proof of its having become putrid, it merely indicates a leſſened difpofition to coagulate; and

do

* Lind's 2d paper, p. 100.
† Lind's 2d paper, p. 87.
‡ Rouppe on the Difeaſes incidental to Seamen, p. 200.

do we not find the blood in feveral other difeafes befides the fcurvy &c. to be in a more fluid ftate than it is in health? Certainly we do.

We are informed by Dr. Lind, that the blood of fcorbutic perfons did not impart the leaft fenfe of acrimony to the tongue, any more than the white of an egg; and that the blood of fcorbutics does not become putrid fooner than other blood, which it certainly ought, cæteris paribus, if it had already begun to putrefy in the body. Nay we are moreover informed by this celebrated writer, that the ferum of the blood of fuch patients, is not fceptic but antifceptic; and would it not be abfurd and inconfiftent with the facts of chemiftry to fay, that a portion of matter which had already began to putrefy on being added to an unputrefied mafs fhould retard the procefs?

The benefit derived from the ufe of frefh vegetables and their acids in curing fcurvy, is, in my opinion, by no means to be admitted as proof of the blood's being in a putrid ftate.

We muft in this place notice, that it is a well eftablifhed opinion, that the powers of digeftion are fuch, as to be capable of converting all matters into one and the fame kind of chyle, whether animal or vegetable, though the one may not afford it in as great proportion as the other.

The above circumftance being admitted, and it cannot be denied, we at the fame time muft allow, that thofe matters undergo a confiderable change in the ftomach before they go on to the formation of the blood. Confequently, if they fuffer a change, they poffefs no longer the properties of a vegetable, or a vegetable acid, and therefore a tertium

quid

quid muſt be formed. What its nature and properties are I will not pretend to ſay, but leave the candid to judge for themſelves; though we might equally well ſuppoſe it to be ſeptic as antiſeptic*.

There are many phyſicians, who ſuppoſed fixed air to be chiefly uſeful when injected into the inteſtines in thoſe diſeaſes ſuſpected to be putrid, by acting as an antiſeptic on the putrid blood; but when, thus applied, does it not rather act on the contents of the inteſtines, and deſtroy the bad effects produced by their offenſive ſmell, &c. ſince it has been well obſerved, " that, any thing putrid is totally incompatible with the perfect well being of the animal?"

It is generally allowed, that putrid effluvia act as debilitating powers on the ſyſtem. Indeed putrid matters, lying for a time in the inteſtines, would ſeem to be debilitating, as in the inſtance of the dyſentery. It appears alſo that fixed air acts as a ſtimulant: Mr. Henry found that it inflamed an ulcer †. And Dr. Dobſon ſays, that when received by the mouth into the ſtomach, in ten minutes, it raiſed the pulſe from 71 to 77 ſtrokes ‡.

It was objected to me, that the urine, breath, and other excretions of perſons labouring under diſeaſes of the putrid

* I think that the following circumſtance juſtifies my aſſertion, that vegetable aliment after it has ſuffered the changes produced on food in the ſtomach, &c. when it is ſent on to form the chyle, has more of a ſeptic than antiſeptic quality. Fordyce on Digeſtion, p. 164, mentions, that by diſtillation in a retort we obtain an empyreumatic oil, volatile alkali and water, and charcoal remains in the retort, whether the ſubſtance diſtilled be chyle, a piece of fleſh, or other animal ſubſtance.

† Henry's Exper. p. 127.

† Dobſon's Commentary on Fixed Air.

trid clafs were highly fœtid and obnoxious. We grant this may be the cafe ; though a queftion will then arife, whether thefe excretions contract this fœtor from the blood, or become fœtid after they are feparated from the general mafs ? I am of the latter opinion, and think it highly probable that they become fœtid in their refpective refervoirs, or in fome other manner not yet explained. We know that the excretions do not by any means poffefs the properties belonging to the blood, and we alfo know that they may be very different in difeafe, though the blood remain the fame as when in perfect health. To this purpofe, I will quote Dr. Home's obfervation—he mentions that the blood of diabetic perfons appeared perfectly natural; that the ferum of the fame poffeffes no more fweetnefs than that of other blood ; though the urine of the fame patients tafted very fweet, and upon evaporation afforded a large quantity of faccharine matter.*

The cafe of a patient, who was lately under the care of my worthy preceptor Dr. Wiftar, may alfo be mentioned in confirmation of thefe fentiments. He was affected with pneumonia, and had all the ufual fymptoms ; but in addition to them, an odour proceeded from him fo putrid and offenfive that no one could remain long in his room without great inconvenience, it even extended its offenfive fmell into the rooms a ftory below him. His urine had alfo an intolerable fœtor. The fymptoms of pneumonia required bleeding, and this remedy was ufed with great caution ; but notwithftanding the above circumftances, the blood coagulated very firmly, and had fome inflammatory appearances on its furface.

2   The

* Homes's Clinical Experiments, p. 332.

The arguments taken from Dedier's, Couzier's, and Homes's Experiments, employed by Dr. Ferris to prove, that the bile and blood undergo a change in the plague and measles, are by no means conclusive. We know the plague and measles to be highly contagious diseases, and easily communicated to those who are in a state of predisposition to receive the infection. Dr. Ferris supposes, that as the blood or bile of one who died of the plague, when injected into the veins of a dog, produced symptoms of that disease ; and as the measles ensue after inoculating with the blood of those who labour under it, the blood and bile must have undergone changes in those diseases. In my opinion these facts prove nothing that favours such a conclusion ; and all that we can infer from them is, that the contagious or infectious matter was diffused through the blood, or adhered to it in those instances, as it does to old buildings, cloathing, &c. Facts prove that it does so with respect to these subjects, for months, nay even years, and then is as effectual as ever in its deadly operation. We are uninformed of the appearance or state of the blood in those instances. In the measles, the blood appears to be no more changed or altered than in other inflammatory diseases. How it is in the plague, I know not. Dedier and Couzier have taken no notice of any evident change—Gentlemen whose accuracy would not have allowed them to have neglected such a circumstance if it had occurred.

What confirms me in the opinion, that the contagious matter was only diffused through the blood, or adhered to it in the same manner as to old buildings, &c. is, that in the one instance the plague, in the other the measles,

K

was

was produced. If the contagious matter had mixed with the blood fo as to produce a chemical change therein, neither the plague nor the meafles would have been the refult of the Experiments; as by this mixture, they would both have loft their former properties, and a new compound would have been produced by their union, not poffeffing the properties of the contagious matter or of the blood. The fixth law of the affinity of compofition, reads thus : " Two or more bodies, united by the affinity of compofition, form a fubftance, whofe properties are very different from thofe of any one of the bodies before their combination."* Confequently a difeafe very different from the plague or meafles muft be produced, if a chemical union had been formed.†.

With refpect to Dr. Home's Experiment, I beg leave to make one or two obfervations : He fays, "I thought that I fhould get the blood more fully faturated with what I wanted, if it was taken from the cutaneous veins amongft the meafles, than if I took it from a large vein, where there was a much greater proportion of blood from the more internal parts than from the fkin. I therefore ordered a very fuperficial incifion to be made amongft the thickeft

---

* Fourcroy's Chemiftry, Vol. I. p. 64.

† We have already proved that the blood in the veffels of living animals was not fubject to the laws of fermentation, and that no fermentation could be excited in it by the introduction of ferments; therefore if a change had been produced in the blood in the above inftances, it muft have been by a chemical union, and confequently muft be fubject to the laws of chemical affinity.

thickeſt of the meaſles, and the blood, which came ſlowly away, was received upon ſome cotton."*

The Doctor appears to be of the opinion that a fermentation of the blood, produced by the introduction of contagious matter into the ſyſtem, was not the cauſe of the diſeaſe; for, he ſays, the blood taken from the more internal parts was not as plentifully ſaturated with the morbillous matter as that flowing in the cutaneous veſſels. Is not this inconſiſtent with the true and well underſtood courſe of the blood? For, is not the blood of the cutaneous veſſels at one moment in one part, and at another in a very different part, of the ſyſtem? Conſequently the whole maſs muſt have been equally affected. Again, if the motion of the blood were not itſelf ſufficient to produce the change throughout the whole maſs, this would have happened from the well known laws of fermentation; for we know that a very ſmall portion of a ferment is ſufficient to aſſimilate a very large maſs of fermentable matter. Further, this experiment is not concluſive, ſince the blood was obtained by a very ſuperficial inciſion made a-mongſt the thickeſt of the meaſles, and the blood alſo flowed ſlowly. Here certainly in making the inciſion, the lancet or inſtrument uſed muſt have pierced ſome of the puſtules from the ſituation in which it was made; and as the blood flowed ſlowly it had time to entangle or mix with a quantity of the matter contained in the puſtules; ſo that this experiment is a very indeciſive one. Moreover I have been told by a gentleman who ſometime ſince attended the Lectures of the celebrated John Hunter, that

* Home's Medical Facts, &c. p. 268.

that Mr. Hunter informed his pupils, that he had made frequent attempts to inoculate with the blood of thofe who had the fmall-pox, and lues venerea, but never fucceeded in imparting the infection.

Lind's obfervations on the blood in the yellow fever fupport the opinion, that fubftances different from the blood may be diffufed through it without changing it. He relates that the ferum was of a deep yellow tinge. A perfon by curiofity tafted it, and found it bitter.*

From thefe facts we learn, that the bile may exift in the blood-veffels, without producing a change in the blood, or fuffering one itfelf, fince its fenfible properties were in thefe cafes evident. Who will affert that the properties of the blood are changed in jaundice?

We might proceed to a much greater length in proving that certain fubftances may exift in the blood-veffels of living animals unchanged themfelves, and without producing any change in the blood, as turpentine, &c. This, I believe, is a pofition at prefent generally allowed by phyficians—I fhall therefore pafs it over in filence.

Eruptive difeafes were, for ages, fuppofed to be owing to changes in the blood; but the following Experiment would feem to operate againft the doctrine. D. Coxe, transfufed between 14 and 16 ounces of blood from the jugular vein of an old dog, who laboured under an eruptive difeafe, into the jugular vein of another dog, who was in health. This being done, the difeafed dog got well; and

* Lind's 1ft. Paper, p. 13.

and to the other, who received the blood which might probably have been fuppofed to be affected, nothing amifs happened.*

This Experiment proves clearly that the blood did not fuffer a change from the difeafe under which the dog at that time laboured. Eruptive difeafes are, I believe, for the greateft part contagious ; and as the blood did not, in this inftance, communicate the difeafe, we cannot fuppofe that the contagious matter adhered to it ; this, therefore, ftrengthens my opinion, and leaves room for the fuppofition, that contagion may adhere to different parts of the body in different fubjects.

If contagious difeafes are produced by the contagion operating upon the blood as a ferment, whence is it that the blood of brute animals is not fufceptible of being excited into this fermentation, fince, from Experiments, it appears to be much of the fame nature with that of the human fpecies ?

Five months after the above fheets were written, I had the good fortune to obtain a reading of Dr. Milman's very ingenious " Enquiry into the fource from whence the fymptoms of the fcurvy, and of putrid fevers, arife, &c." wherein the author difplays a great deal of ingenious reafoning. I was happy to find that we agreed in fentiment refpecting the general opinion, though we have treated of the fubject in a very different manner. For particulars I refer the reader to the book itfelf.

Thus I have fought in nature the phœnomena of my doctrine. In my own eftimation, facts refpond to theory,

† Etmulleri Opera, Tom. 3tio, p. 1619.

ory, and the inferences of my Experiments to fpecula-
tion. When I firft contemplated this fubject, I was not
particularly attached to any opinion refpecting it; and,
from this circumftance, I gained the advantage of an im-
partial and unprejudiced examination of facts. After
collating and confidering the Experiments I had made,
I drew my conclufions with a deference to reafon. If,
in the event, I fhall have contributed to advance the in-
terefts of Medicine, and furnifhed any principles to aid
the labors of practice—to leffen the horrors of putrid
difeafes—and to arreft, for a moment, the dreadful arm
of death, I fhall be more than compenfated for performing
my duty, and paying this tribute to humanity.

T H E   E N D.

www.ingramcontent.com/pod-product-compliance
Lightning Source LLC
Chambersburg PA
CBHW030004030726
47499CB00008B/2892

*9 7 8 3 3 3 7 3 9 4 8 5 1 *